THE CAT-TAILED RABBIT AND OTHER STORIES

Translated from the Original Chinese

THE CAT-TAILED RABBIT AND OTHER STORIES

FAIRY TALES FROM TANG TANG

TANG TANG

Illustrated by
LÜ QIUMEI

Translated by
LI XIAOCHUN

Edited and Adapted by
REBECCA MOESTA

Creative & Translation Consultant
DENNIS JI DING

EBook ISBN: 978-1-68057-303-9
Trade Paperback ISBN: 978-1-68057-302-2
Hardcover ISBN: 978-1-68057-304-6
Casebind ISBN: 978-1-68057-305-3
WordFire Press Edition 2022
Cover design by Janet McDonald
Cover artwork images by Lü Qiumei
Library of Congress Control Number: 2022935395
Published by WordFire Press, LLC
PO Box 1840 Monument CO 80132
Kevin J. Anderson & Rebecca Moesta, Publishers

CONTENTS

ONLY TWO INCHES

Two inches away ...
Snap!
Squeak!
A puff of light smoke,
When the wind comes,
Turns into wisps,
Dissolves into air,
Never to be found.
Only two inches,
Only two inches.

Every little imp in Ball Imp Valley sang this song. Ball Blue hummed softly as he stepped out of his ball-shaped house, pulled a tiny tape measure made from grass stems out of his pocket, and measured straight ahead of him. Two inches away stood a wild lily with dewdrops on several petals. He shook the stalk, raised his chin, and let the droplets fall into his open mouth.

Dew is the only food of Ball Imps.

Not far away, Ball Purple was drinking dew from a hyacinth. She also stood two inches from her ball-shaped house, feeling a little bored.

Ball Imps were not supposed to go more than two inches from their own ball houses. Every imp in the valley knew this rule.

Only two inches, no further.

But beyond two inches what would happen? "Two inches away ... *Snap! Squeak!* A puff of light smoke, when the wind comes, turns into wisps, dissolves into air, never to be found. Only two inches, only two inches." Wasn't the answer in the song?

Whoops! Ball Purple looked at her wristwatch. Her nineteen seconds was almost up! She ran back into her house as Ball Blue dashed back into his.

Ball Imps are not supposed to leave their ball houses for any longer than nineteen seconds. But after nineteen seconds, what would happen? "Two inches away ... *Snap! Squeak!* A puff of light smoke, when the wind comes, turns into wisps, dissolves into air, never to be found. Only two inches, only two inches." Wasn't the answer in the song?

The blue ball house rumbled and rolled upward, and the purple one rumbled and rolled forward.

"Not good!" they cried almost in the same instant. Instantly the two houses stopped, exactly six inches away from each other.

It was exactly six inches—take their grass rulers and measure it if you don't believe me. The imps themselves are always measuring, and their eyes are as sharp as their rulers.

No ball house in the valley is allowed to be within six inches of another. Any closer than that, and "*Snap! Squeak!* A puff of light smoke, when the wind comes, turns into wisps, dissolves into air, never to be found." Wasn't the answer already in the song?

Normally they would have switched directions and rolled their houses apart, but today they both chose to stick their heads out of their tiny little windows.

Blue saw Purple. She had a pair of very long lashes that fluttered like the wings of a butterfly.

Purple also saw Blue. He had a mark like a star on the left side of his brow.

The inhabitants of Ball Imp Valley look much like we do, except that they are an inch or so tall, plump and pink, and have very round faces and huge eyes. Purple's hair was purple, and Blue's hair was blue, which matched the colors of their ball-shaped houses.

Purple's eyes glinted, and she cried, "We—we seem to have been born together."

Ball Blue shook his head. He didn't remember the day he was born, when he and his house rolled down the rock together. Who knew how long or how far he rolled? He stopped in a place where there were many white ball-shaped houses rolling and hopping around, but none of them paused to take care of him. After a long time, a hoarse voice sang,

> Two inches away ...
> *Snap!*
> *Squeak!*
> A puff of light smoke,
> When the wind comes,
> Turns into wisps,
> Dissolves into air,
> Never to be found.
> Only two inches,
> Only two inches.

Who on earth would sing such a horrid song? Blue looked out his window and saw a red ball house with an open window.

A wrinkled face appeared in the window. "Remember, remember! No further than two inches! No longer than nineteen seconds! No closer than six inches between ball houses! And take a ruler with you, take a ruler."

Later, Blue learned that she was the oldest imp in the valley, and taught every newborn imp her song, which explained the hoarseness of her voice. Purple had taken her classes too.

Ball Imps have no mother or father—they are born from a big rust-colored rock above the valley. After the first spring rain of each year, several balls no larger than a grain of rice emerge from the rock and grow a little with each subsequent rainfall. When the seventeenth spring rain ends, the balls start rolling downhill, and the little imps fall asleep inside, as they roll right into the arms of Ball Imp Valley. If there are fewer than seventeen rains in spring, however, the balls all shrivel up and disappear. And as we know, very few springs have as many as seventeen rainfalls. Unsurprisingly, the number of Ball Imps is quite small.

Purple, who had kept her eyes open when she rolled downhill, saw a small blue ball house roll past her. She tried to chase after it, but it disappeared very quickly, and she did not find it again.

"You've really never seen me before?" she asked anxiously.

Blue continued to shake his head.

"We were still born together, anyway. I'm Purple!" Purple got overexcited and quickly rolled forward, frightening Blue, who hastily retreated.

"Please keep your distance!" He sounded rather panicky.

Purple paused. "Oh ... right. We'll disappear."

The blue and purple ball-shaped houses stayed six

inches apart, and the two imps poked their blue and purple heads out from their respective windows.

"Why is there a star on your forehead?"

"It's a scar. I knocked my head on the doorframe."

"That's a very pretty scar." Purple's face was full of envy.

Blue laughed. "You're so funny."

The two of them talked for a long time. Well actually, they yelled. Since they had to keep six inches apart, it was hard to hear if they spoke softly. They shouted to each other even after their voices became hoarse, until at long last they could only see each other's mouths opening and shutting.

Perhaps this was why Ball Imps so seldom spoke to each other—it was far too exhausting. Thus, solitude had become the most common way of life for them. They kept both joy and sadness to themselves. And their best friends were their rulers.

"Are you happy?" Purple shouted.

Blue yelled back, "I don't know!"

"Do you ever feel lonely?"

"I don't know."

"Do you get bored very often?"

"I have no idea."

"Why don't you know *anything*?" Purple shouted.

"I know I have to drink dew every day, I know I can only venture two inches from my house, I know I'm not supposed to stay outside longer than nineteen seconds, and I know that our ball-shaped houses have to stay at least six inches apart. Don't I know enough already?" Blue asked.

Purple gave a discouraged sigh. "Oh, my."

"..."

Tired from talking, Blue and Purple took a nap in their own houses and gave their voices a rest. They awoke at the same time, poked their heads out of their windows and began chatting again. But speaking this way took too much effort, so Purple came up with a good idea.

The doors of their houses faced each other, so they opened their doors at the same time and each walked two inches toward the other. Then they were only two inches apart and talking was much easier. But they soon found that this method also had problems, since they couldn't leave their houses for more than nineteen seconds at a stretch and walking back and forth took four seconds. That left only fifteen seconds for talking.

"I don't think the life of a Ball Imp is all that interesting," Purple began.

"Why?" Blue asked from two inches away.

Purple said, "There are so many rules, and—"

She was only halfway through her words when Blue gave the time warning. "Quick, time to go!" So they both turned and ran into their houses, rested for a second, then darted back out again until they were two inches apart.

"What were you saying?" Blue enquired.

"I was running—I forgot," Purple answered.

"I forgot, too."

"I want to touch the star on your forehead," Purple begged.

"Okay."

Purple reached her hand out, but their time was up and they hurried back into their houses.

They ran back and forth, but Purple was never able to touch the star on Blue's forehead. Even though they were only two inches apart, her arm wasn't half that long. There was nothing to be done.

"Do you believe that song is true?"

"I guess so."

"But I've never seen anyone turn into smoke and dissolve into air," Purple said.

Blue answered, "That's because everyone is so careful. They all carry their rulers."

They ran back and forth to continue their conversation.

There was really not enough time to talk, so Purple came up with another idea. "If we run a little faster and cut our time to only one second out and one second back, that leaves two extra seconds for talking, doesn't it?"

Ah. There wasn't any better idea, was there?

"Ready." Blue and Purple stood in their doorways,

crooked their legs, leaned forward, and bent their arms. "Set. Go!"

They ran so fast they heard only the wind past their ears, so fast they couldn't stop. When they finally managed to halt, Purple had run smack into Blue's house, and Blue had crashed into Purple's.

They had gone further than two inches.

Two inches away ...
Snap!
Squeak!
A puff of light smoke,
When the wind comes,
Turns into wisps,
Dissolves into air,
Never to be found.
Only two inches,
Only two inches.

They froze. It was too awful for words—to turn into smoke and dissolve without a trace? It was just too dreadful to imagine. Fear gripped them tightly, and together they shut their eyes. One second, two, three ...

Their eyes slowly opened. They looked at each other, waiting quietly, waiting for their houses to disappear with a snap and themselves to vanish with a squeak.

One minute, two, three ...

They stepped forward and slowly walked toward one another, until they were half an inch apart. Purple touched the star on the left side of Blue's forehead, and said with satisfaction, "There, I did it. In fact, even if we disappear, it's not so terrifying, is it?"

Blue agreed. "I'm not afraid."

One hour, two, three ...

Perhaps they wouldn't disappear after all. They walked hand in hand through the tall grass.

One day, two, three ...

They really hadn't vanished! They walked hand in hand through Ball Imp Valley.

One month, two, three ...

Every day, more ball houses followed them. At last the other Ball Imps came out of their little houses and, one by one, walked further than two inches.

But why did nothing awful ever happen, not even a little bit? What in the world was going on?

Remember that oldest Ball Imp with the rattling voice? She got it all wrong—the song was supposed to go like this:

Two inches away ...
Snap!
Squeak!
A puff of light smoke,
When the wind comes,
Turns into wisps,

Dissolves into air,
Never to be found.
Only two inches,
Only two inches,
Is not very far—keep going.
Go further—it's really all right!

You see, she had completely forgotten those last two lines.

Ha! How could there be such a strange song in the world? Of course, there must be—otherwise what would the Ball Imps sing?

NEVER FORGET

I

At midnight, while the moon glistened white in the sky, on the topmost floor of the city's highest building, a grove of thin trees grew at a visible speed. In a twinkling they grew into a dense forest, with dark tree trunks and shiny leaves. Ancient, gloomy ballads drifted from between the branches and leaves, flowing like strands of silk into the endless expanse of night.

Not far away a boy leaned on his windowsill, staring up in awe. He was called Xiangmu.

A girl appeared on the edge of the tall building's roof. She waved at him energetically, then spread her arms and took a flying leap off the edge.

"Ah—" A cry was halfway out of his mouth when the girl turned into a large white bird in midair, flapped its wings, flew onto his windowsill, shook itself twice in the moonlight, and turned back into a girl again.

"That's my forest," the girl said. "Do you want to go see it?"

Xiangmu stammered, "Oh, Niannian ... I did not know you were a bird ... I didn't know you had a forest."

"You don't like me as a bird?"

"You're a bird ... what a surprise!"

"But I'm *not* a bird."

"Then what are you?"

"Neither a girl nor a bird. Do you want to see what I really am?"

"Yes, please! You are my best friend."

"Then come sit on my back." The girl turned again into a large white bird and flew with the boy on her back toward the roof forest.

II

Xiangmu had known Niannian since he was very little. Ever since he was old enough to remember things —around the age of three. From the day his parents first made him sleep in a room alone, they focused on turning him into a real man. Niannian came into being that day. They grew up together, but Xiangmu never knew anything about her except for her name.

No one else ever saw her either.

It is said that many children have imaginary friends

when they are young. They could see each other, talk, and play together. That's why Papa and Mama thought Niannian was an imaginary friend called into existence by Xiangmu.

"No one else believes that you exist, not even my father and mother," he sighed.

Niannian's lips curved. "Who needs them to?"

He often woke up for a few minutes at around midnight, and Niannian would appear. That's how it was for him, from age three to eleven. Sometimes they chattered nonstop, sometimes they didn't say a word. They were always happy. Niannian spoke very little, but Xiangmu talked all the time. She knew every one of his joys and woes, but he never knew any of hers. Xiangmu asked her once where she came from, why she came only at night, and how she got there—

But she shook her head, saying, "Now is not the time to tell you," and that had been the last of it.

"You will grow up one day," his parents said, "and when you get past the age of imagination, Niannian will go away."

Worried that Niannian would leave him, Xiangmu asked, "Will I just not see you someday?"

"If you don't want to see me, I won't be visible," Niannian said.

"I hope you will always be there."

"Then I will always be here."

This was the highest rooftop in the city, and Xiangmu had seen a forest grow from nothing with his own eyes. Now he alighted in it as though dreaming. Niannian suddenly disappeared.

He walked around exploring on his own. Niannian had brought him here, so there was no need to be afraid. The forest floor was thick with fallen leaves, as if they had been building up for centuries. Large and small trees crowded together, covered with moss, and vines hung from one tree to another. Flowers and wild mushrooms were all over the ground, and a pale mist lingered between the branches.

It was so quiet it felt like another world, and for some reason Xiangmu felt as though many things lurked in these woods, deliberately staying silent. He walked and walked but never reached the edge of the forest. He heard someone humming a mournful and moving song, a song that made the woods feel ethereal and lonely.

Following the sound, Xiangmu came to a huge tree that must have been at least seven or eight hundred years old. It was still full of vitality, its trunk smooth and straight, its crown like a canopy, and its branches seemed to reach right up to the moon.

Niannian's voice came to him. "I am here, Xiangmu."

"Where? I can't see you."

"I am the tree in front of you."

"So you are a tree?"

"To be precise, I am the guardian of these trees. Humans usually call us forest spirits, and I am almost eight centuries old."

Eight hundred years? Xiangmu was taken aback. He had always thought of Niannian as being the same age he was.

"Were you singing just now? It was so beautiful."

"Yes, that was me, singing to my forest. But I cannot sing as well as I once did. I have been sad for too long."

With a rustling of branches and leaves, the girl Niannian stood before him once more, and the ancient tree was gone.

"Am I dreaming?" Xiangmu asked. "Why are you so sad?"

"How is my forest?" Niannian asked.

"It's amazing—but why have I never seen it before?"

"Because it is not for the human eye to see. Because the time has come that I wanted you to see it."

"The time has come?"

"Yes."

"Will I be able to come back here?"

"Do you want to?"

"Of course."

Niannian instantly changed back into the huge tree and said, "Then climb into my branches, break off a thorn, prick your finger, and leave one drop of blood. From then on this forest will remember you."

Xiangmu did not hesitate to do as he was told.

A drop of blood welled up, grew larger, and—*plink*—left his finger and fell to the forest floor.

IV

The moment the droplet reached the ground, the tree shook. The entire forest shook.

It was too late to make it to the ground, so Xiangmu quickly caught hold of the branch nearest to him, as his body was flung from side to side.

A strange noise resounded through the woods, as if released suddenly after being caged for a long time, rushing left and right, wild and chaotic. Every flower and leaf and blade of grass and insect seemed to scream, the uproar pouring into Xiangmu's ears and making his eardrums throb with pain.

The tree shook harder, and he was about to fall when a thick vine dropped from a high branch and tied him securely to the tree trunk.

He didn't understand what was happening, but he kept calm because panic was useless. He called out to Niannian a few times, but his voice was drowned out by the other voices, and he could not even hear himself. Opening his eyes wide to look at his surroundings, he saw all the trees twisting, and the ground writhed with countless gray roots, thick and thin, that swished as they grew, crawling like snakes.

He could not see any further since his sight was blocked by dense leaves and branches. He could not see those countless roots spreading like water in all directions, flowing down from the roof over every wall and every floor of the apartment complex. Before dawn, they enveloped the entire building.

The people in the building heard the strange swishing sound, looked out their windows, and broke into a cold sweat. Running outside, they looked up and saw that the roof of the building had somehow become a dense forest, and the roots hanging down from above kept crawling toward the earth. When the roots touched the hard, cold pavement, they crept across it, and wherever they encountered cracks, they burrowed down with ease.

Touch the mud, touch the earth, touch the soil, and find rebirth ... Xiangmu thought he could hear Niannian saying.

Countless roots touched the earth deep beneath the city and the soil gave them boundless new energy. Roots sprouted from roots, and each root thrived under the earth.

People could actually hear the roots spreading through the soil, and the sound quickly spread to every corner of the city. It sounded as though myriad rivers were flowing underground, and myriad angry snakes were crawling. The earth began to shake, and so did their houses. Everyone escaped from their homes and evacuated the city.

At noon a pale sun hung overhead, and the hard ground throughout the city cracked and crumbled. An endless sea of roots broke free of the ground. Full of energy, growing wildly, they climbed up the buildings and encircled house after house.

At dusk, as if on command, they began to squeeze. They tightened around a house. The house cracked and collapsed. Bricks and tiles rained down. *Boom*. And *boom*, house after house fell, raising enough dust to blot out the sun and sky.

By the time the moon rose, not a single house was left standing. The last to fall was the tallest building. It buckled like a giant collapsing to its knees and became an enormous pile of sand and rubble.

The trees on the roof seemed to grow feet and scattered to the corners of the night. Smaller trees grew longer roots, and when they met the wind, they sent their roots further down through steel and concrete, deep into the earth.

The city no longer existed. Not a person was in sight. Bare trees with long and twisted roots rode on the ruins, high and low.

Xiangmu still clung to a tree above the remains of his home. His parents were nowhere to be found. The vine loosened and he tugged it off. He jumped down and landed on roots as gray and thick as pythons. The world was deadly quiet. His eardrums began to throb again. Had it all been a bad dream?

V

Many, many years earlier, the city had been a beautiful forest. It had lasted for a long, long time—no one knew just how long. The guardian of the forest was a gentle, innocent, carefree wood nymph.

Then, thirty years ago, a group of people came there and refused to leave. Within three to five years, the forest was gone, replaced by a patchwork of houses and apartment buildings.

The nymph was homeless. Reluctant to leave, she wandered the area year after year.

She never stopped missing her forest, never stopped dreaming of taking it back from the humans. She called herself Niannian as a reminder: never forget, never forget.

On nights when the moon was fullest, on the topmost floor of the highest building, she would sprinkle a handful of seeds from bygone days. Humming a sad little song, she grew them into a forest, but the trees only lasted while it was dark, and only she could see them.

At daybreak, the forest faded into nothing, and Niannian burst into tears each time the woods disappeared.

Wasn't there any way to stop them from disappearing? There was, but it would require human strength and a willing sacrifice of one drop of blood.

In the world many wood nymphs had lost their forests, and most of the nymphs were older than Niannian. They stayed in place, wandered aimlessly, or gathered in small groups and combined their powers to make humans miserable. They invited Niannian to join them, believing her efforts were a waste of time. The forest on the rooftop meant nothing. They had once done as she did, holding on to the illusion of their dead forests and weeping until their hopes broke.

"Your powers are too weak to grow a new forest," they told Niannian. "And you'll never bring your forest back all by yourself."

But Niannian waited for that drop of human blood. For her forest she would wait as long as it took. She wandered the city day and night, sometimes as a leaf, sometimes as an insect, sometimes as no more than a speck of dust or a glimmer of light.

Xiangmu's house occupied the exact spot where Niannian had once stood. She had returned there quite often since losing her forest. She saw Xiangmu born. As she watched him grow, a plan sprouted in her mind, and he was its most crucial aspect. She decided to become his closest, dearest friend, and ask him to shed blood for her forest.

One year passed. Another year passed. Niannian waited patiently.

Today was the day she had waited for. She had finally rescued her forest from the humans. She had done it—the forest was the meaning of her existence!

For a long while she stood motionless, simply savoring the wild happiness inside her.

VI

Xiangmu cried out—for Papa, for Mama, for Niannian.

Niannian was right beside him in the form of a tree. Of course, she could hear him, but she did not want to reply. She had done what she needed to do, and Xiangmu would soon move elsewhere with his parents. There was no need for them to see each other again.

He patted the tree trunk. "Niannian? You *are* Niannian, aren't you?"

Niannian held her breath and kept quiet.

Xiangmu stood before her a while, then hung his head, turned, and stumbled away.

She watched his unsteady figure as he picked his way through the rubble, and she couldn't help herself— they *had* to say goodbye, at least.

She turned back into a girl. "Xiangmu!"

When he saw Niannian, he burst out crying. "Do you know what in the world is happening?"

"I do," Niannian said.

"Can you tell me?"

"I can."

She could have refused to explain, or simply lied to him, but she couldn't bring herself to do it. Xiangmu had asked, and she wanted to be open and honest. She had done nothing wrong and had nothing to hide.

Xiangmu listened to her story, his face white as a sheet, his body shaking as if he had been hit hard.

"Then ... it was my blood that helped you destroy the whole city?"

"You could say that."

Xiangmu stared at her with tearful eyes and balled his hands into fists.

Niannian looked straight into his eyes and did not shy away. "Do you hate me? I didn't do anything wrong. I simply took back what you took from me. You gave me pain, and now I'm giving it back to you."

Xiangmu opened his mouth, but only one word came out. "I ..."

She cut him off quickly. "You are one of *them*."

"You ..." Xiangmu felt as if a ball of thorns had been shoved into his chest.

"*I*? I am not to blame." Niannian gave him a frank look. "The only thing I am guilty of is lying to you for a drop of blood."

He stopped speaking and did not look at her. He started to stagger away.

She suddenly thought of something. "Come back, Xiangmu!"

Xiangmu paused but did not turn around.

"Will you bless us before you go? My forest needs your blessing to become beautiful again. Otherwise it will always be ugly."

He stood for a moment without looking back, then continued on his way.

Niannian's voice called to him over and over until it faded out of his hearing.

VII

Xiangmu moved with his parents to another city.

He never made another friend. He never trusted anyone. His heart was always cold. He lived alone, grew up alone, and little by little became old.

He tried hard to forget Niannian, but he could never forget. He couldn't forget how he used to wake up in the dark and see her the moment he opened his eyes, how the starlight and wind followed her into his room, how much he always had to say to her.

Time flowed, and he gradually found that he did not hate her so much. In fact, she had done nothing wrong by taking back her woods.

He just couldn't be happy anymore.

Niannian had her forest, but her happiness did not last. Her forest grew over the ruins of a city, filthy, chaotic and lifeless. Roots exposed to the air crawled like gray pythons across her line of vision. No grass ever grew, no flowers bloomed, no mushroom sprouted. Not a single animal came—not a bird or snake or bug.

She closed her eyes to block out the sight. There could be no uglier woods in all the world, and she could do nothing to lift her spirits.

She often thought of Xiangmu. She had expected to forget him quickly. She remembered how they had leaned on his windowsill together, counting stars, enjoying the breeze together, laughing together. She was happiest when she thought of him. How close they had been, and how fond Xiangmu had been of her. Such memories always made her feel a bit better.

As the years passed her longing for him grew stronger and stronger, so strong that it made her weep with sorrow. She felt as if a hole had opened in her heart, and not even a forest could fill that hole.

Will he ever come back? she thought. *If he did, I wouldn't beg for his blessing, I simply couldn't ask again. It would be enough just to see him. But how could he ever come back?*

Whenever the wind blew between the sky and earth, Niannian felt it pass straight through the hole in her heart, and its bite was sharp and cold.

VIII

Xiangmu returned.

He was no longer a boy but an old man. He stepped cautiously through the ruins of the city and over the tree roots, walking toward her step by step.

Niannian stood and stared. She wanted to cry. She wanted to laugh. She wanted to say a thousand things to him, but she couldn't say a single word.

Xiangmu patted her trunk. "Niannian, is that you?"

She burst out crying, and all of her leaves rustled. She had never expected to cry. It was rather inappropriate for a wood nymph.

Xiangmu waited quietly for her to finish.

"I am so happy ..." she said. "I thought I'd never see you again ... Why did you come back?"

"I am cold. I am growing weak. Soon my legs won't be able to walk a step."

"I can see that."

"I was afraid that if I waited any longer I wouldn't have the strength to come back and do it."

"Do what?"

Xiangmu opened his arms wide and hugged her trunk. "I'm here to bless you and your forest. May you live in beauty and peace forever."

Niannian burst into tears again.

"Perhaps I should have come sooner," he said. "Now I should go home."

"Why did you come?" she cried. "I can't believe you really came back!"

"Because we were the best of friends," he told her in a low, calm voice. "That will never change."

"Can you stay, then? I will make you young again—I'll take you back to your youth, and everything in this forest will be yours! I'll never lie to you again …"

"I must be going."

"We will be happy together!"

"There is no going back to the past, Niannian. Goodbye."

Xiangmu left, as he had many years before. He walked very slowly and never looked back. He thought of how Niannian had appeared as little girl when he was a little boy, and he smiled at the memory.

A gentle rain started to fall in Niannian's forest. In the rain, grass grew, and mushrooms grew, and flowers bloomed.

Many years passed, and lush vegetation embraced the city ruins. Together, many people visited the forest. All who ventured in were amazed by its strange beauty, and many wept when they saw it.

GRANDMA HIDING IN MY TEETH

I

"I am looking for Fang Suyun." His speech was rough and rude and thoughtless. He had appeared suddenly and silently in front of me.

I was afraid. After I gathered my wits, though, I was simply indignant. In an angry voice, I said, "Who? I don't know her."

"Of course you do," he insisted.

I raised my voice. "Of course I *don't*."

"You're lying!" His words were louder than mine. "Fang Suyun is your grandmother—how could you not know her?"

Was she my grandmother? I never knew that her name was Fang Suyun. I only knew her as Grandma. So her name was Fang Suyun? I couldn't help but repeat it a few times. "Fang Suyun, Fang Suyun."

He got rather impatient. "Yes, that's who I'm trying to find!"

"A few years ago, my grandmother left this world forever," I said. No matter how much time passed, mentioning her always felt like reopening an old wound.

"I know that," he said with a wave of his hand.

He *knew* but was still looking for her? I was confused. "And you are ...?"

"I am Death," he answered slowly.

Death? Shocked, I jumped back several paces.

He did look a bit strange, now that I thought of it. Dressed in a flowing blue-green robe, he had a straw hat pushed back over his shoulders and a long, flowing beard. In his right hand he held an emerald-green flute.

"You're joking, aren't you?" I asked.

"There is no world in which Death likes to joke," he answered solemnly.

"But ..." I had to admit, he looked nothing like Death as I had always imagined him. No black robes, no ghostly features, no dark hood or skeletal face.

"I like to dress up as a respected authority figure in the world, so that I look awe-inspiring enough to be an immortal, yet elegant enough to be dashing. A good balance, don't you think?" he said. "Don't call me Death. Call me ... Cold Westerly Wind."

To me, the name didn't feel imposing enough for Death. *"Cold Westerly Wind?"*

He gave me an inquiring look. "Yes?"

Actually, I hadn't been talking *to* him, just trying out the name to see how it sounded.

"God doesn't like my new name at all, but I love it to the bone—so chilling, so poetic."

Even though he didn't look frightening, I couldn't help but shiver. "You ... are you here to take me away?"

"No, I'm not interested in you—for now. I'll come for you when you're eighty-nine."

"Then you ..."

"I said, I'm looking for Fang Suyun."

"Didn't you take her away several years ago?" I asked quietly.

"I did, but this morning she slipped away from heaven and came back here," Cold Westerly Wind said, very much annoyed.

"Slipped back here?" I exclaimed with delight.

He nodded. "Yes, and if I don't find her before sundown, God will take it out of my paycheck!"

Death's paycheck had nothing to do with me. My heart was pounding so that it almost leapt out of my throat, but it was because of my grandmother. *Grandma, are you really back?*

"She didn't appear to you?"

"No."

"Didn't talk to you?"

"No."

"Or stroke your hair?"

"No."

"Oh, I must be going mad!" Cold Westerly Wind rapped the flute sharply against his own head. "After all, how would she dare appear to you? How would she dare speak to you? Your soul would be on its way to heaven by now if she did. She wouldn't dare!"

Is that so? I thought. *Then Grandma must be hidden in some corner right now, watching me!*

Cold Westerly Wind muttered to himself. "It's so strange! No one can hide from Death, so why can I not find Fang Suyun? Would she come here first thing? Or would she go somewhere else? But she told me herself that she loves her granddaughter above all.... Enough, enough, I may as well look somewhere else. Slower, sun, set a little bit slower!"

Whooooo. Cold Westerly Wind blew into his green flute and floated away, playing a string of notes that did not form a tune.

II

As soon as he was out of sight, I set my voice free and eagerly shouted, "Grandma! Grandma!

"Grandma, where are you?

"Grandma, come out quick.

"Grandma! I've missed you so much!"

I kept yelling as I searched for her. I climbed under the bed. I opened the big closet. I ran my hands over every inch of space that might hide someone. But I could not see her, could not touch her, could not tell if she was here.

"Death isn't here anymore, Grandma, you can come out!" I kept searching frantically, almost in tears. *Grandma, my plump Grandma, you've been gone almost five years. Do you know how I've missed you? It hurts so much that my mind is blurry, and I can't remember what you look like anymore.*

"Stop hiding, Grandma!"

I was shouting myself hoarse when Cold Westerly Wind—Death—reappeared.

He was all smiles. He even had shallow dimples near his mouth.

My heart quaked. "You ... did you find my grandma?"

"No, but I know where she is hiding." He looked disturbingly happy.

"Where—where is she?" I asked nervously.

"In your teeth, without question," Cold Westerly Wind said. "Every escapee from heaven must hide in the teeth of the one he loves the most, or else Death will see him," he continued. "See how forgetful I become when I'm anxious? I completely forgot."

I shut my mouth tight without realizing it.

"Open your mouth."

"No!" I shook my head.

But Death quirked his little finger at me, and my mouth opened of its own accord.

I mumbled, "I won't let you take Grandma away!"

Ignoring me, he poked his long green flute into my mouth and started tapping my teeth.

"Not here."

"Not this one either."

"No."

"Nor this one."

"Still nothing."

"…"

"Unbelievable!" Cold Westerly Wind exclaimed once he finished tapping all my teeth. "Nothing here. How is it possible? Aren't you the one she loves the most?"

He hung his head and got ready to leave. Before he left, he turned and said to me, "Your grandma is an idiot!'

"She is not," I retorted crossly.

"As stupid as can be!"

"Watch who you're calling stupid, stupid!" I refused to be polite to anyone who called my grandma stupid— no matter who it was.

"Stupid enough to assume that she can get away with this!"

"Didn't she do that already?" I argued.

"Oh, I'll find her. Cold Westerly Wind will find her."

"You haven't—yet."

"Sooner or later," he said. "And then she will be punished."

"Punished?"

"Yes. Severely."

Death told me that God had decided to require every soul that went to heaven to plant cactus for five years before it could become an angel. "Cactus planting is no fun. They are spiked all over, and the spines poke people all over. It's painful and itchy and itchy and painful—just *miserable*.

"Squeezing between cacti all day long, your grandmother gets poked more than anyone else. She is also quite afraid of pain. Every night she sits on the edge of the bed and cries while pulling out cactus spikes. She cries so many tears that the water comes up to her ankles."

Grandma! My heart hurt as if it had been stabbed all over by cactus spines.

Death smiled coldly. "Your grandmother will be assigned ten more years of cactus farming now."

"Ten years? How will she stand it?"

"Well, she shouldn't have left! It's heaven—nobody should want to get out!"

"What if you never find her?"

"Ha! You must think me very stupid, little girl,"

Death said. "There is no soul that Cold Westerly Wind cannot find."

"Oh, dear Death, please don't punish Grandma so badly if you do find her!" I had never pleaded so earnestly with anyone.

His face froze. "What did you call me?"

"Oh. Cold Westerly Wind."

"That's more like it." He smiled and nodded. "Cold Westerly Wind—what a beautiful name! But God makes the rules, and I can't do anything about it."

"Please, O great and terrible Cold Westerly Wind, please stop searching!"

"No, that's not possible. I'll tell you what an idiot she is—she only needed to plant one more month of cactus, and she would have become an angel, free to walk between heaven and earth," he said. "Sadly, now she'll have to plant cactus for ten more years—what a setback!"

Once he was finished, Cold Westerly Wind raised his flute and floated away. *Whoooooo!*

Hide well, Grandma!

III

Upper teeth, under the bed
Lower teeth, up overhead
Nothing silver, nothing gold
Only mouse teeth

Small and old.

I ran breathlessly for two hours and arrived at the house where Grandma used to live.

Grandma's house had been locked for several years, and no one but me had been there since she left. I had secretly kept a key. When I missed her, I would run for two hours to get there, if only to wipe her tables and drink from her big white china mug. Or, better yet, lie on the bed thinking of her plump arms and plump face.

Grandma's bed was made of finely carved wood, with a frame that looked like a little cabin when the mosquito netting was pulled down. I always slept with her, until the day she got sick.

She was sick for almost two years.

When she first became ill I was seven, and my baby teeth started falling out. Every time a tooth came loose, she would sing, "Upper teeth, under the bed, lower teeth, up overhead. Nothing silver, nothing gold, only mouse teeth small and old."

My new teeth were small and white, and for all her weakness, Grandma was as pleased as a child. "Oh, oh! See how useful my song is." From the moment my first baby tooth was thrown under the bed, she never let anyone clean beneath it again.

I was nine when all my teeth grew in.

She sometimes woke, opened her bleary eyes, stared

into my face, and mumbled, "How could I ever leave you?"

Soon she closed her eyes.

Soon they locked the front door.

After that, there was no Grandma in the house.

I have no memory of my mother. She left when I was barely a year old. Papa was so filled with grief that he could not care for me, so I grew up with Grandma.

With Grandma gone, my father took me into his home. There was a stranger there, however—a new mother. She was very polite and proper. She never spoke to me in a loud voice. After she had a son, she had little time to spare for me.

I ran to Grandma's house every few days and left with my heart a little warmer.

I bent down and crawled under the bed. It was dark there, and thickly layered with dirt. I felt around carefully with my hands. One, two, another ... ten teeth in all.

I got a stool and stood on tiptoe to feel around on the canopy, raising large puffs of dust that gave me a rattling cough. One, two, another ... ten teeth in all.

As I stared at the handful of teeth, the strains of her song seemed to echo in my ears. I could see her face again: pale eyebrows, plump lips, a plump nose, and large front teeth that showed whenever her lips widened in a laugh.

My tears pattered down and blossomed like wet flowers on the ground.

"Grandma! Grandma!"

She had to be hiding in these teeth, but all my calling could not make her answer. I knew she must be in there, even if she stayed silent!

Perhaps she was asleep. Perhaps what Death said was true and she couldn't speak to me. I slipped the teeth gently into my pocket and lay down on the wooden bed, humming,

Upper teeth, under the bed
Lower teeth, up overhead
Nothing silver, nothing gold
Only mouse teeth
Small and old.

I kept humming and humming. Suddenly I heard,
Uh ... uhh ... urrp!
Uh ... uhh ... urrp!
It sounded so familiar! Wasn't that Grandma burping?

It *was* Grandma burping! She loved to drink strong tea out of that big china cup, and she liked to burp. I could never forget those two things. In fact, her burps were spectacular—almost like singing.
Uh ... uhh ... urrp!
The burping sounds were coming from my pocket.

Grandma really was in my teeth! I felt so dizzy with excitement I could barely breathe. I pressed my hand tightly against my pocket.

Grandma, Grandma! I was slightly calmer after half a minute. I scooped all of my teeth out of the pocket and held them in the palm of one hand.

"Did you really sneak back here, Grandma?"

Uh ... uhh ... urrp!

"I've missed you so much."

Uh ... uhh ... urrp!

"Grandma, don't go away anymore!"

Uh ... uhh ... urrp!

"I am always lonely, Grandma."

Uh ... uhh ... urrp!

"Grandma, please promise me."

Grandma kept burping no matter what I said. Papa once called her tendency to burp an illness. I was surprised that her years in heaven had not cured her.

But at this moment, I was happy just to hear her burp.

IV

I was still basking in bliss when Cold Westerly Wind suddenly floated down from the roof in his blue-green robes.

He cocked his head and muttered, "I've thought this through, and Fang Suyun must be close to you. There is no one else here for her to love—your Grandpa and mother are already in heaven."

His presence alarmed me. I somehow forgot to stick my hand back in my pocket and raised my fist instead.

"What is that in your hand?" Death asked.

"No ... nothing." Flustered, I hid my hand behind me.

"Nothing, truly? Children shouldn't lie." His eyes stared into mine.

I gave my head an exaggerated shake and asked in a trembling voice, "Have you found my grandmother?" I was hoping to distract hm.

"No," Death said, "but I will soon enough."

Uh ... uhh ... urrp!

Oh my God, Grandma was burping again!

"What was that?" Death asked.

Uh ... uhh ... urrp!

I quickly burped as well. "Nothing. It's just me."

"Ha, ha. You?"

Uh ... uhh ... urrp!

Uh ... uhh ... urrp!

Nothing could stop Grandma once she started burping. It was always like that, and all I could do was burp as hard as I could.

Death laughed out loud. "It seems you can burp a duet." His arm stretched out with a *swish*, snaked behind me, and retracted with a *swish*—leaving my hand empty.

"My teeth—my teeth!" I sprang at him heedlessly.

"You'll get them back, no worries," he said in a bland voice.

As I lunged at him again and again, he drew a circle around me with his flute. Suddenly I couldn't move.

Death smiled. He spread my teeth out on his palm and began tapping them with his flute, one by one.

Bang. "Nope, not here."

Bang. "Nope, not there."

Bang. "Darn. Not there either ..."

The burping stopped at some point. Had Grandma fainted? Or had she somehow escaped?

Run, Grandma!

Bang. "Nope, not here."

Ka-BANG. The last tooth he tapped made a strange sound.

"Aha! Ha-ha-ha-ha!" Death waved his flute wildly overhead, his eyes wide, his eyebrows raised. "Found you, Fang Suyun!"

I went weak in the knees and sank to the floor on my rear end.

"You can have them back now." The handful of teeth leapt from his hand, sailed in a graceful arc through the air, and settled one by one in my coat pocket.

V

In my eyes there was only Death, no Grandma.

"Where is my grandma, Cold Westerly Wind? Why can't I see her?" I asked anxiously.

Death chuckled. "If you could see her, that would mean you were on your way to heaven."

"Grandma!" I called out as loud as I could.

"Don't waste your breath. Your grandmother can't talk to you. If she says a single word, I'll have to take you too—God's rules."

"Grandma?" What did I care if Death took me? At the moment, I only wanted to hear her speak. Even if she said just one word—my name, a promise, an answer —I would be satisfied.

Death said, "Oh, she really wants to talk to you. Her face is turning as purple as a pig liver, but she doesn't dare speak."

"Grandma—" I started to cry.

Death was impatient. "Stop shouting. I need to have a talk with Fang Suyun. Don't interrupt us."

He faced me, lowered his head, and seemed to talk to the air right in front of me. "See, Fang Suyun? You couldn't get away, could you?"

I realized that Grandma must have been standing face to face with him, so I reached out hoping to touch her, but my hands met empty air.

"Yes, I knew I couldn't," I heard my grandmother say, in her usual low, slightly hoarse voice.

"Grandma—" I couldn't help but cry out again.

"One more word," Death warned, "and I'll seal your mouth shut." Then he continued talking to Grandma. "If you knew you couldn't get away, why did you sneak out?"

"I missed my granddaughter."

"Didn't you know what would happen if you left without permission?"

"Yes."

"Then why?"

"I missed my granddaughter."

"Aren't you afraid of another ten years of cactus farming?"

"I am afraid."

"Afraid, yet you dared to run?"

"I longed to see my granddaughter."

Cold Westerly Wind shook his head. "You are a fool, Fang Suyun. You were so close."

"I didn't think about it. For the first time in all these years, you had forgotten to lock heaven's doors. I just took the opportunity! I couldn't waste an instant."

"Grandma," I sobbed, "you idiot!"

"Well then, Fang Suyun, time to go back to heaven and start planting cactus," Death said. "Thank God the sun hasn't set yet!"

"Grandma!" I wanted to hang on to her arm or the hem of her skirt like I did when I was a child. "Grandma, I can't see you!"

Death began to play his flute, a sound painfully out

of tune, and he floated up. My invisible grandmother must have floated up with him.

I sat on the ground and cried hard, even harder than I had cried when I was nine and Grandma died.

To my surprise, Cold Westerly Wind came back a short while later. "Your grandmother beseeched me mightily for a chance to speak with you."

I sprang up. "Please let her!"

"All right, I will allow it. God is always telling me that I'm too soft-hearted for Death, you know."

"Thank you, Cold Westerly Wind!"

"But each sentence she speaks will cost her one more year of planting cactus."

Another whole year? Oh, no! I shook my head desperately. "In that case, I don't want to speak to her at all."

Grandma spoke to me. "You little Villain, you refuse to hear your grandma talk? I've spent so many years loving you, I know you miss me. Sadly I've been so busy cactus farming that I haven't even had a chance to visit your mother or Grandpa. I'll come see you again, little Villain!" Grandma's voice was right beside my ear, soft and bubbly. She had always called me Villain, which made me angry, but she had explained that she used it as a special name to show how much she loved me. I didn't understand it back then. Now I did.

"One, two, three, four. Four sentences is four years. Oh, all right, all right—let's call it one year," Death said.

"You must never sneak out again, Grandma."

"But what if I can't stop thinking of you? What if I miss you so much I can't stand it?"

Death held up two fingers. "Two years."

"Grandma, I don't want you to come back at all!" I hardened my heart and did my best to sound cruel. "You would scare me."

"I wouldn't scare you, little Villain—I would just watch you quietly."

"Three years." Death raised a third finger.

I was getting angry at him. "Get out of here and take my grandmother with you! And from now on, please don't forget to lock your door!"

"Little Villain!" Grandma's voice was incredibly tender. "You've grown as tall and beautiful as your mother was. Is—is *she* good to you?"

"Very, Grandma. Don't worry, she never scolds me at all." I tried to sound bright and happy. Oh, how I wanted to admit that my stepmother kept me at a distance with her polite, aloof demeanor, so that I could plunge into the warmth and comfort Grandma would offer.

"Four years." Death held up a fourth finger.

"You look very well. Ah, I feel much easier in my mind."

"Five."

"Oh, heavens. Stop talking, Grandma!"

"Villai—"

"Enough, Fang Suyun!" Death said majestically. "Stop talking. This is about much more than farming cactus."

Grandma's voice suddenly stopped.

Then Death looked at me with damp eyes and said, "I don't know what happened to me. But listening to you, the ice in my heart melted, as if by a fire. I won't tell God about those five years."

"Thank you so much, Death!"

"*What* did you call me?"

"Er, thank you, Cold Westerly Wind!"

"Come, Fang Suyun." The Cold Westerly Wind of Death disappeared from my sight. They were gone, though the strange music of his flute lingered.

I turned toward the sound of his flute. *Please, Grandma. Please don't ever sneak out again!*

THE CAT-TAILED RABBIT

I

When I was young, I once visited a place very far away.

I caught a cold that day and began sneezing nonstop. After one gigantic sneeze, my vision went dark, my ears rang, and my body swayed. When I regained my senses, I stood in a strange place on a vast expanse of gray. The wind blew so hard it lifted pebbles into the air.

An old woman in a dark headscarf hobbled toward me, hunched over a cane. She had a sharp nose and chin, and cold eyes.

I asked her hastily where I was and what had happened.

"You are in the world of fairy tales," she said.

"How could there be a world of fairy tales?"

"How could there not? This world has existed since the first fairy tale came into being."

"Don't be ridiculous! Even if there were a fairy-tale world, it wouldn't be like this."

She cackled so hard that her body trembled all over and gave off a smell like rotting sweet potatoes.

I wrinkled my nose. Actually, she did remind me of an old witch from a fairy tale.

"As you can see, I am an old witch," she said, and I stared at her in shock. She cackled again, sounding like a nest of rats was scrambling around in her throat.

The skin on my scalp and heels tingled.

"You're luckier than most to be able to come—you're also more *un*fortunate than most. Nobody asked you to sneeze when Xixi did, so here you are. Now, ahem. Let me clear up the matter once and for all: the fairy-tale world is half wilderness and half paradise. The name Paradise is self-explanatory, and the Wilderness is rather dreadful for you humans."

"Shouldn't a fairy-tale world be all Paradise?"

"You must not have read many fairy tales if you say such silly things! There is a balance. If there is day, there is night, if there is warmth, there is cold, and if there is happiness there is sorrow. So it is with the world of fairy tales. Congratulations, and welcome to the Wilderness!"

"I don't like it here. I want to go home now."

"That's not for you to decide." The old witch cackled and handed me a cloth bag. "Now go find gold in the riverbed. You can go home when you've filled this sack." It was large enough to hold a medicine ball.

"Tell me your name."

"Cici," I said reluctantly.

The face of a rabbit suddenly peeked out from behind her wrinkled neck, stuck its tongue out at me, and ducked out of sight.

II

It was a really dreadful place.

Wasteland, desert, rocky beaches, swamps, bare mountains and dark forests, with a heavy gray sky hanging over everything. The ground crawled with thorny plants that poked at me and made me bleed. Lurking among the plants were strange creatures that sometimes darted out to bite my ankles.

A sluggish yellow-gray river wound through the desolate land, stirring up pus-colored foam. And I would have to extract an entire sack of gold from the river before I could leave.

Every day, the old witch gave me a bowl of dark gruel. I was so hungry that sparks rose before my eyes, and my front stuck itself tightly to my back. I never saw anyone else except for the old witch. At night, I curled up and slept in a dirt hole that was dark and damp, and my teeth chattered.

Only one thought occupied my mind: gather gold to

fill the sack as quickly as possible and get out. Every day before dawn, I bowed and stepped into the cold water. I scooped up handfuls of rock and sand from the riverbed and searched for tiny glimmers of gold. I returned to shore only when it got too dark to see. My neck and spine were close to breaking, my eyes swollen with tears, but the gold in the sack barely covered its bottom.

I cried for the old witch to have mercy and send me home, but she said, "You agreed to this the first day you came here, so how can I change anything? You will go home when you've filled this sack with gold. I will never break my word."

"Why are you doing this to me?"

"It relieves the boredom—heh-heh."

"There isn't enough gold, and this sack is much too big … I'll never be able to fill it."

"Then you'll never leave."

I lay in a stupor at the edge of the river for several days and nights. I no longer had the strength to get up. Perhaps it would be better to fall asleep and sleep forever, than to live in endless fear and despair!

III

A furry paw tickled the soles of my feet. I opened my eyes to see a fluffy white ball at my feet. It looked like a rabbit. Its red eyes stared at me as it hopped up to my face. My head was half-buried in the sand and my hair looked like a bird's nest.

It said, "Get up."

"You can't make me," I answered blearily.

"I have something good to eat."

"I'm not eating anything." I shut my eyes lazily, but the aroma of fresh bread wafted into my nose, and something soft touched my lips. I bit down on it, and my tongue and teeth trembled with delight. I wolfed the bread down, nearly nipping the rabbit's paw with the last bite. I swallowed the entire loaf in a twinkling, burped with contentment, and then felt embarrassed that I had behaved like that in front of a rabbit.

"Now you have strength to get up," it said.

I rolled over, turning my back to it, my face burning.

"I can help you," it said from behind.

My heart bounded with joy, but I said, "I don't believe you. You're just a little rabbit."

"I am the old witch's rabbit. There are many things I could help you with."

"She wouldn't let you help me."

"Then I won't tell her."

"But she is a witch—she has her ways."

"I am the old witch's rabbit. I have ways ... to keep her from finding out."

I turned so that the rabbit and I were face to face. "Why would you help me?"

"Because I brought you here."

"*You're* the one who sneezed?" I sat up at once.

"Yes, a midge flew up my nose," it said, looking sheepish. "It was my first time sneezing. I didn't know what would happen."

I stared into its eyes. "Then you must help me!"

"I will," it said, hopping onto my knee, and I saw that it had a tail like a cat.

"You ... are you a rabbit?"

It lifted its white tail decorated with black stripes, saying, "I think cat-tailed rabbit would be more precise. It's a gift from the old witch. She says it makes me look special. But of course, you could call me Xixi if you wanted—that's my name."

"Xixi—our names sound so alike."

"Our names will always make people smile," Xixi said. "Hello, Cici." Its lips curled at the sides to reveal two big white teeth, and I laughed.

It had been a long, long time since I laughed.

IV

Xixi proved to be a ray of light in my darkness, a fire in the winter cold, a handful of water to quench my thirst ... and that isn't an exaggeration.

It sneaked to my side whenever the old witch slept. The old witch fell asleep as soon as the sun set and remained comatose throughout the night, getting up only when the sun was high. She took long naps after lunch and slept until dusk without a break.

Xixi gave me bread from the old witch's table to fill my belly. It dug a larger hole for me and lined it with dry grass. At night it nestled close to me like a hot little stove, and its soft fur smelled like warm honey. It left only at dawn, and each afternoon it came into the river to help me pan for gold. It dove like a fish to the bottom of the river and soon resurfaced with gold in its paws. It comforted me with its small thin voice, saying, "Don't worry, Cici, you'll go home soon."

One day Xixi did not come, nor the next day, nor the next. Starving, I searched all over for it by day and curled up shivering at night.

On the fourth day it reappeared, and I hugged it tightly to me and cried, getting tears and snot all over its fur.

It turned out that the witch had taken it to Paradise to enjoy the fairy-tale world's festivals, and from the celebrations Xixi brought me many sweet things— cookies and candies and chocolates and delicacies by the dozens.

All that day I whimpered, "Please don't leave me, Xixi ... please don't ever leave." I had never been so deeply attached to anyone, not even my parents.

"Please don't ever leave me, Xixi ... please stay forever."

Xixi swished its cat-like tail while its red eyes stared into the distance.

V

Gradually the sack filled with gold, until it was so full to the brim that the mouth of the bag could not be closed. Then I delivered it to the old witch.

"Can I go back now? Will ... will you let me go home?"

The old witch didn't even look at it. She tossed the sack into the river with a wave of her hand, where the fine gold sprayed from the bag and disappeared into the water.

I cried out in horror. "You—"

The old witch dusted her hands off. "What are you worried about? You think I'll go back on my word? Hah. This is the fairy-tale world, where we all have to keep our promises. You can go back, I'll allow it. Just sneeze once and ... Wait! How did you do it? How could you possibly have gathered a full bag of gold so fast? Tell me, tell me!"

Xixi peeked out from behind the old witch's neck and blinked its red eyes at me.

"You don't want to tell me?" Her wrinkles gathered from the outside of her face toward its center, until her nose puckered like an old pinecone. "Heh, if you don't tell me, I'll see it in your eyes."

"Granny, Granny, Granny!" Xixi jumped down from its perch on the old witch's neck and into the crook of her arms. It reached out with a small paw and gently batted the witch's nose, making her giggle.

"Aye, my precious little darling, my sweet little darling, my gorgeous little darling, what is it? Say anything you like, and I'll like everything you say."

In a precious voice Xixi said, "You'll keep your word, won't you, Granny? I heard you say that you'd send her back once she gathered a sack full of gold. Or have you forgotten?"

The old witch giggled. "Yes, yes, Xixi is right! I shan't ask a single word. You go home now—sneeze and go home."

"Can—can I stay for one more night?"

"What, you like it here so much you don't want to leave? Heh-heh, of course you can, and I'll let you eat bread from my table, too! You can leave whenever you like, but I warn you, don't upset my darling Xixi—my little Xixi has quite the temper."

VI

I stayed because I wanted to take Xixi with me. I liked it.

I sat by the river waiting for it, and it bounded toward me in the night like a fluffy white ball and fell right into my lap.

"Aren't you going home, Cici?" it asked. "Isn't this the day you've been waiting for?"

I hugged it. "Will you come with me?"

"To where?" Xixi stretched its neck out from the crook of my am.

"Home. My home." I stroked its long tail.

Xixi shook its head. "My home is here."

"It's not good if you stay here—I swear you'll like my world better, you'll like it ever so much."

"Is it nice there?"

"Very. There are tons of pretty things to play with, and good food everywhere."

"But Paradise also has pretty things to play with, and good food everywhere, and the old witch takes me there often."

I rested my chin on Xixi's head and began to cry, because I couldn't bear the thought of never seeing it again.

"Are you crying, Cici?"

"Yes, I am. I want to stay with you forever."

"I don't want to be apart. But I don't want to go anywhere either."

I began to cry louder. "Please come with me, Xixi, come with me! You don't know how much I like you!"

Xixi started crying as well. "Don't cry, you're

making me sad ... Okay, I'll go ... but I'm afraid. I don't know what will happen in the future. Will I ever be able to come back? I don't want to leave the old witch."

Something flew up my nose, itching fiercely. "Ah-choo!"

Everything went dark, there was a humming in my ears, and my body swayed from side to side. When the world settled again, I was sitting on my own bed with Xixi still in my arms.

Its red eyes swiveled around frantically, its body trembling like a leaf.

I leaned down close to its ear and whispered, "Don't be afraid, Xixi—I am here. I'll be very good to you, and you'll be so very happy—I promise. Trust me. Trust me."

Xixi couldn't stop trembling for a long time.

I was so happy I had brought Xixi to my world!

VII

I had spent a long time in the fairy-tale world, but it turned out that in my own world only a few hours had gone by. When I told my family excitedly what had happened to me, they smiled and said what a nice daydream it was.

Xixi hid in a drawer and refused to come out, no matter how much I begged. It also refused to eat. I worried over it day after day, taking little food and sleep, until I got blisters on my lips.

"Come out, Xixi! Eat something, you'll starve."

After many days, it came out and got into my arms.

"You must be good to me," it said sweetly.

"I'll be very good to you," I promised, stroking its head.

"Then I will be very good to you. I don't change."

"Neither will I."

"You mustn't tell anyone."

"I swear I won't breathe a word."

Slowly Xixi began to move about the room. It hid in the coverlet and under the bed and in the closets. After a time, it hid in my backpack when I went outside. I took it to school, to the playground, the cinema, and the park—it followed me wherever I went. We were together almost every second.

"Your world really is a great deal of fun, Cici." Xixi's bright red eyes were clear and shining. Everything it saw filled it with wonder. "Thank you so much for bringing me here."

The ice cream and strawberry cake I loved quickly became its favorite. We lived together happily enough and were almost inseparable.

But I also made it angry sometimes without meaning to.

One day I was almost late for school, and in my rush I forgot to pull Xixi out from beneath the covers and put it in my school bag. By the time I came home from school, it had been crying all day under my bed. I picked it up tenderly, but it scratched my face in a fury. My tears rolled down as I apologized profusely and promised that it would never happen again.

Its red eyes got even more red as it sobbed, and if it hadn't been afraid of being overheard, it would have burst out bawling. "You must always be with me," it repeated. "You must always be at my side—remember, or I will be afraid."

"Yes, I'll remember," I said again and again.

We were always together. At home, I only had to tell Papa and Mama that I was going to study, shut the door and lock it, and they would never dare disturb me. I carried my school bag everywhere I went. Xixi became so timid that it insisted on staying close enough to hear my breathing and hear my voice. It had to nestle close to me just to fall asleep. It depended on me just as much as I had depended on it in the fairy-tale world.

Once, I was having so much fun with a group of girls in the park that I left my backpack on the lawn for a long time.

Xixi was furious with me and said it wasn't fair that I had so many friends when it had only me. I agreed that it seemed unfair. To placate Xixi, I began to shut myself off from my other friends, though I loved playing with them.

Another time, a neighbor boy asked me to go to the river with him to pick up stones. I didn't really want to bring Xixi along, but it pouted and refused to be left behind. There was no other choice but to take it along.

Sometimes I really needed to be alone. Sometimes there were secrets I needed to keep for myself. Xixi didn't care. It always said, "Don't leave me for a minute. Don't leave me even for a second."

I couldn't let Xixi feel alone. I was the one who had brought it here, so I did my best to care for it, satisfy it, listen to it. Xixi's dependence on me wrapped around my heart like sticky spider silk. Although it could get burdensome and a little annoying, how much inconvenience was that compared to the comfort Xixi had once given me?

VIII

One night, I dreamed that the old witch had arrived from the fairy-tale world to take Xixi back. We said goodbye to each other, waving happily. I was still waving when I woke up and found Xixi crouched close to my head.

Its honeyed scent found its way into my nostrils as it said, "You are neglecting me more and more. You went out three times without taking me along, and once you watched TV in the living room for two hours straight before coming back in. If you keep this up, I'll leave you. I'll have the old witch come pick me up."

"You mean she can take you home?" I was surprised.

"Of course she can." Sounding like a little girl, it snorted, hummed, and tilted its head to one side. "All I have to do is stand by the window and lift my tail and she'll come take me away, and then you'll never see me again."

"If you just raise your tail?"

"Of course—my tail was a gift from the old witch, and it can send out an amazing signal. Do you want me to show you?"

I hugged it close to my chest. "Don't."

It crouched on my chest and muttered, satisfied, "Remember, Cici, I only have to stand by the window with my tail raised, and you will never see me again."

Time passed, year after year, and I entered high school. Xixi grew bored with everything the world had to offer, and focused all its attention on me. I, on the other hand, grew ever busier, and became interested in many more subjects, while my school workload steadily increased. By comparison, Xixi was only a tiny part of my life, and its dependence on me—sticking like glue— often made me feel smothered.

And what a cross, whiny, irritable, wild, and unrea- sonable rabbit it was! I gradually forgot how Xixi had looked and acted in the fairy-tale world, and I could hardly see anything cute about it at all. When I didn't put up with its behavior, we quarreled and said hurtful things to each other.

Sometimes I deliberately "forgot" to bring it when I

went out, and it never jumped into my backpack of its own accord. It always waited for me to carry it around like a princess, just to hold on to its pitiful pride in front of me. Once I got home, it coldly ignored me or lost its temper and messed up my room and kept me awake all night. I was so frustrated that sometimes I wanted to grab it by the ears and throw it out the window.

One night I lay crying softly on my bed, and Xixi woke from its dreams, reached out with its paws and wiped away my tears. It asked me what was wrong, but I didn't say a thing. If I explained, I would break its heart, and possibly make a mess of my future life.

As it turned out, my fears were unfounded. Xixi soon decided to leave.

A harsh wind was blowing that day, and my heart was pounding with worry about an important exam. When I went out that morning, I didn't want to bring Xixi along, but it stared at me with huge, tearful eyes, until I gave in and put it in my schoolbag. During the exam, it stuck its paw out of the bag several times and scratched my leg. The exam problems were difficult, and with Xixi distracting me every few minutes, the results were not surprising. The grades came out that after-noon, and when I got my test paper back from the teacher, I wanted to crawl into a hole in the ground.

My mood was dark and terrible, and I threw my backpack on the floor as soon as I got home. Xixi crawled out and stared at me angrily.

I said, "Let the old witch come and pick you up."

"Really?" it asked.

"Really."

"Do you hate me?"

"I can't stand you anymore."

"You clearly said you wanted to be together forever."

"That was before."

"Then why did you ever bring me here?"

"I regret it now."

"All right," it said. "Goodbye, then." It jumped onto the windowsill, stared at me with its red eyes, raised its black and white tail straight up like a flagpole, then somersaulted out of the window and disappeared.

The wind blew back the scent of honey. I stared blankly for a moment before rushing to the window. Outside, a wilderness of long grasses rippled in the wind. I called out "Xixi!" several times, but there was no reply.

The old witch had come and taken it back.

I sighed. I felt relief mingled with indescribable loss.

I did not see Xixi again after that.

IX

I grew up, graduated, got a job, and became the mother of a little girl. Behind our house grew a wilderness of lush grass, with all kinds of delightful bugs and flowers. My daughter Axun loved to play there.

One day at dusk, she returned from the fields smelling faintly of honey. I couldn't remember what it reminded me of, only that the scent was familiar.

I vaguely understood that Axun had a secret. Her eyes sparkled with mystery and delight. I asked her what she had found, and she said, many things—bugs and flowers and butterflies and tiny wild berries.

She spent more and more time in the fields, and she often took delicious food with her. Once I heard the door opening in the middle of the night, and I got up hastily to see Axun walking out the front door.

"It is late—where are you going?"

She paused. "I ... I wanted to see the moon." A thin white crescent hung in the sky.

I said, "Come back inside. You can see it from the window." Despite her reluctance, she retraced her steps, and I gave her a light tap on the head. "Don't sneak out at night. It's dangerous, you know?"

I watched her retreat into her room, then got back into bed and lay down. Her father had slept through everything, yet I could not for the life of me fall asleep. The faint scent of honey I had smelled on Axun trickled like a thin stream into the depths of my memory. I followed it and found—Xixi!

Yes, it was Xixi's fragrance. How could I forget? I had asked it once why a rabbit would smell like honey. It had shaken its head in confusion, then said that the old witch liked honey.

Was Xixi back? If so, why had it come to Axun instead of me?

She had been so secretive recently, running out to play in the wild fields whenever I wasn't paying attention. Had she been with Xixi? When she tried to sneak out tonight was it because of Xixi? My heart stuttered and all the unpleasant memories came flooding back. My life was busy and stressful. I didn't want Xixi to cause trouble—for me or Axun.

The sound of the door opening reached my ears again. Axun must have thought I was asleep and decided to sneak out again. I held my breath, waited until the door closed, and then got up.

I followed as she jogged all the way. It was an autumn night with a chill in the air. Axun crouched down in a patch of dog's tail grass, and I inched closer to her. When I was only a dozen steps away, however, she stood and turned toward me, holding something white and furry in her arms as she walked closer.

"Xixi has been sick, Mama, sick for several days, and I don't know what medicine to give it. It wouldn't let me tell a soul, but now its eyes won't open and it may be dying."

I didn't know why my heart was pounding so fast, and I took a couple of steps back.

Xixi lay in Axun's arms, its long cat's tail hanging limp, almost bald.

"Let's go home first, Axun."

X

We placed Xixi on the sofa. It seemed to be asleep, its ears drooping, its tail limp.

Axun told me that she had been playing outside one day when she saw a rabbit dragging a long tail and chased after it. It moved very slowly, one hop at a time, and she pounced on it.

From beneath her it had said, "Lighter—you're hurting me!"

She was so shocked that she rolled off at once, and that was how they met.

Perhaps it was the living room's bright light that opened Xixi's eyes. It looked at me for a long time without saying anything.

I said, "What's the matter, Xixi? Go back to the old witch, quick—surely she'll be able to cure you."

"All right," it said. "Just let me raise my tail first." But only the tip of its tail moved slightly.

Then its eyes slowly closed, and we could no longer hear it breathing.

Axun burst into tears. "Do you know what a forlorn rabbit Xixi was, Mama? It came from the fairy-tale world, and it was sick when we met—how else could I have caught it so easily?"

I felt a flutter of guilt, as if a sick butterfly trembled inside me. "Did it ... did it tell you how it came here from the fairy-tale world?"

"Yes, something about being too brash while playing one day. It slipped out of its world and could never get back."

"Did it say who brought it here?"

"No, it came by itself."

"Is ... is that so?"

I slid from the sofa to sit on the floor. *Xixi!* It had not gone home. It couldn't get back to its own world ... The old witch hadn't come to pick it up. It had always been here, so close to me ... All these years, how had it managed? Why had it lied to me? And why hadn't it told Axun the truth?

I know why. I know.

"Xixi—"

When you say "Xixi" your lips widen gently to the sides and tilt slightly upward. The little rabbit had told me that our names, Xixi and Cici, would always make people smile.

PUBLISHER'S NOTE

The original text of this work was created in Chinese. The translator, editor, and publisher have made every effort to ensure that the English-language version is as accurate as possible and in keeping with the artistic intent of the author. Because this work reflects a different culture, some of the ideas and attitudes may be unfamiliar to the English-language audience.

ABOUT THE AUTHOR

Tang Tang, one of China's most celebrated authors of children's literature, began creating fairy tales in 2003. Her works often integrate traditional Chinese storytelling with Western fantasy elements, using vivid and humorous language to craft unique stories of wonder and magic.

She is a member of the Chinese Writers Association (and one of its first "National Reading Promoters"), vice chair of the Zhejiang Writers Association, and image spokesperson for reading in Zhejiang. Tang Tang has won numerous children's literature awards in China, including the Gold Award. She has won the National Outstanding Children's Literature Award—China's highest award in the field—for three consecutive years.

Among her best known works are "Hiding in Your Heart," "Kakasha the Water Sprite," "A Biography of the Incisor A Shang," and "Green Pearl." Her works have been translated into English, Japanese, Russian and many other languages.